GHETTO

QUEEN

CORDERO DIAMOND

ISBN: 978-1-970135-57-2 Paperback
       978-1-970135-58-9 Hardcover
       978-1-970135-56-5 Ebook

Published in the United States by Pen2Pad Ink Publishing.

Requests to publish work from this book or to contact the author should be sent to: corderodiamond@gmail.com

Cordero Diamond retains the rights to all images.

Ghetto Queen

CONTENTS

Dear You,

My name is Deja. Before you tune in to read a portion of my life story, I would like to inform you that this story takes place in the early 2000s: Long before the presence of transgenders or homosexuals were even considered being tolerated in the Black Community and long before we had any rights. This story takes place in a time where you had to hide your identity to be safe. If you were found out, you could possibly be killed.

Yes, I know there are still many hate crimes happening to the LGBTQ community today, but we've come so far from where we were when this story took place. Things are no longer as rough as they were when I was younger. Back then you had 2 choices that guaranteed your survival: be happy and fight for your life or be miserable by keeping it a secret and staying safe. Today, we no longer hide who we are though some still choose to do so.

To my LGBTQ family of age, I know the fight isn't over yet, but at least there is still a fight. To my young LGBTQ family, know that it will get better with time. When all else fails remember this quote from the famous author **Dr**. **Seuss:** "Be who you are and say what you feel because those who mind don't matter and those who matter don't mind."

And to my hetero family, you may not understand us. Still, please try to be mindful that no matter who we are, what we are, or who we choose to become that we are all not only someone's son/daughter, grandson/granddaughter, but we are all human beings. We all want to be loved, and we all want somebody to love. Being different is what makes us all individually special and shouldn't make a person any less than the next. Homosexuality is found in many species. Homophobia is found in just one. I love you all, and I hope you enjoy!

Sincerely,

Ra'Deja Shawntel Saxton

A LITTLE KNOWN
SO FAR

Growing up in the ghetto
praying to succeed with a dream.
Trying my best to show others
I can act, write, dance, and sing.
But it gets so hard day after day
trying to be known.
When you have no money and you have
no fame, your dreams are usually slept on.
But I won't give up
cuz I know my chance is coming.
So, I sit, and I write down this poem.
And now that you've read it,
you know that I said it.
And that makes me
just a little more known.

CHAPTER 1

FAREWELL

"Gay boy, gay boy! You need to be in Playboy!" Tears streamed down Deja's face as she reminisced some horrible childhood memories while doing 90 on the interstate. She had recently turned 18 and was finally free to do whatever she pleased. Deja had struggled with her sexuality since she was about 10 years old. Even though her mother was incredibly supportive, her 3 younger brothers weren't. She fought them just about every day because of how disrespectful they were, and she was so tired of it. They would do things like call her Jermain (her boy name) in public, introduce her as their big brother to their house guests or clock her tea in front of trade!

Deja began her transition at age 15. You would think that the boys would have accepted her by now, but they weren't going for no fag as their big brother. To them, the shit was embarrassing!

Now, she was a gorgeous, dark skinned, tall drink of water with long thick wavy hair. Most people assumed she was mixed with some other ethnicity because of the texture and length of her hair but that wasn't the case. Deja was 100% black. As a boy, she already had a very feminine body, so the hormones she was prescribed just softened up her large bubble butt along with developing her a perky C-cup breast. She hadn't had any work done to her body yet, and she didn't plan on having anything done. In her eyes, her body was perfect. Deja was very passable as a woman, and most people would have never guessed that she was born male. She was leaving Louisville, KY where her family currently resided and was headed back to her hometown Rockford, IL where she would stay with her cousin until she got on her feet.

Deja was on a quest for life, love, romance, and happiness. There was no way she would be able to pursue any of that around her family, so a fresh but familiar start was in order. Deja continued to reflect on the memories as she drove. She remembered the time she came out to her family as gay. She was 12 years old when she decided to call her family down to the living room. Scared but extremely excited all at the same time, this moment would be one she would never forget.

"I know you're all wondering what this is about. I have something to tell you. For the past two years, I've been tryna figure out who I am, and I think I finally got it."

"Can you get to the point?!," Jaycion, her little brother blurted out.

"If you'd shut up and be patient I will!" Deja snapped. "Any way, I've been struggling with trying to figure out who I am, and I finally got it. I am Jermain, and I am gay!"

Jaylen, Deja's other brother, burst into tears. Jaycion and Jasper sat in complete silence. Their mom was the first to speak.

"Baby, I knew you were gay at the age of five, I just wasn't ready to accept it. You are my baby. I will love you no matter what," Her mom responded.

"Well, I don't want no faggot as my big brother," Jasper snapped.

"You betta watch yo' mouth!" their mother shouted.

"Nah Ma, fa' real. Don't nobody want no sissy as they big brother." Jaycion butted in.

"Jaycion! Jasper! That is your brother. No matter what, he will always be your brother. You will not disrespect him! If I catch you disrespecting' him, I'ma beat y'all ass! You hear me?" Momma said.

"Yes Ma'am." They both replied in unison.

In the beginning Deja's brothers never disrespected her in the presence of their mother. When she wasn't around, all hell broke loose in the disrespect department. Time progressed and the impudence became worse. Once she began her transition, even their mother couldn't control them. So, Deja and her mother agreed that once she was of age that Deja could leave without warning. They both had been putting money aside for this day since Deja was 16, and today was the day. She had packed up all her things and hit it without even as little as a goodbye! Deja looked in her rear-view mirror, wiped away her tears and continued to punch it down the interstate. "Goodbye Louisville!"

CHAPTER 2

WELCOME HOME

After a long 4 ½ hour drive, Deja had finally made it to her hometown! Rockford look so different now. It had been 5 years since she had been home, and things had changed a lot. *I guess I wasn't the only one who had a transformation over the years,* she thought to herself. She drove around the south, east and north side of Rockford. By the time she was heading to her cousin's house, she noticed her gas light had popped on. She headed to a Citgo gas station a few blocks away from her cousin's house.

Suddenly, her car began to tremble and slowly came to a stop. *Shiiiit!,* she yelled to herself. Deja didn't know what to do. She panicked. The car stopped right in the middle of the street. Her 2007 Ford Focus wasn't big at all, but she knew she couldn't push and steer it to the side of the road all by herself. And leaving her car in the middle of the street wasn't an option. Deja put her hazard lights on, threw the car in neutral, and started to push as hard as she could. The car barely moved an inch, but she kept pushing. Then, out of nowhere, the car began rolling and felt light as a feather. Deja started to feel a bit of relief only to notice that there was a man behind the car pushing. He was about 6'1, light skinned with freckles covering the cheek parts of his face. He had a muscular build, his hair was jet black, and he was rocking a low-cut Caesar with deep waves. He wore glasses that made him look very educated, but even with glasses she could tell he was a thug. He was very attractive, and she was relieved to see him.

"Hey Shorty. Hop in and steer it off to the side!" the man yelled to Deja. Deja did exactly as she was told. Once the car was off to the side of the road, she threw it in park and jumped out.

"Thank you so much." Deja said.

"Dam shorty. What you do? Run outta gas?" he said tired and out of breath.

"Yeah," she replied. "I thought I could

make it to the gas station over on Concord, but I was wrong. Thank you again, by the way. I was havin' a rough time pushin' this thang by myself."

"I saw you," he said smiling. "I couldn't stand by and watch a shorty as sexy as yourself just struggle like that. That's not what's up. I'm Omar."

"I'm Deja." she said reaching out to shake his hand. She paused an extra couple of seconds to embrace the feeling. It sent shivers down her spine.

"You got a gas can, Deja? If you don't, I got one. I can give you a lift to the gas station. It's only a few blocks away." He asked.

"Yeah, I got one." she replied. Deja popped her trunk, grabbed her gas can, and made her way to Omar's truck. Omar had an all-black Dodge Durango with tinted windows. It was decent but needed to be cleaned out. She could tell he smoked by the Swisher Sweet wrappers and blunt guts that seem to have been wasted on the floor. The faded aroma of kush and cologne that filled the truck turned her on. Deja didn't smoke, but she loved guys that did. It was something about a hood nigga that did something to her.

He was hood as fuck, and she wanted him on sight.

"So, what chu doin' in Rockford?" Omar asked.

"Movin back from Kentucky." She responded.

"They got black people in Kentucky?!"

"Not many. And definitely not many like me."

"I believe it. Your flyness is rare." Deja blushed at Omar's remark.

"Thank you. So, what do you do? There has to be a reason for these muscles" she asked playfully touching his arm.

"I work for my brother. He owns a chop shop on Riverside." He responded. Deja's eyes softened. That was a huge plus in Deja's eyes. She wasn't a gold digger, but Deja wasn't checking for any broke niggas. No doubt she was a sucker for a thug, but a broke thug didn't stand a chance with her.

They arrived at the gas station, and Omar decided to fill up both gas cans. Then, he took her back to her car and emptied both cans into Deja's car. She sat in his truck watching. She knew it didn't cost much to fill up both cans, but the fact that he did it without knowing much about her was another plus. She was really attracted to Omar, and she could tell the feeling was mutual. Before she got out of his car, she called her phone with his phone to store his number. Once he finished, she got out of the truck and attempted to start her car. It choked at first, but, on the second try, it cranked right up. Deja was so ecstatic that she hopped out of the car and jumped into Omar's arms. Omar wrapped his arms around her waist.

"Dam Shorty! If you get this excited over getting a little gas, then I need to fill you up every day!"

"If I let you fill me up. Gotta earn that privilege Playa." She kissed his cheek said Thank you." Then, she got in her car and sped off. She saw him in the rearview completely still and stunned. She smirked. Deja knew exactly how to keep niggas thinking about her. Omar hadn't seen the last of her. She was not finished with him...yet.

CHAPTER 3

DUDE LOOKS LIKE A LADY

Deja finally finished unpacking all her things. She had been staying in the Concord Commons Housing Projects with her cousin, Leah, for about 3 weeks now, and it was not going so well. Leah's crib was filthy! She had mice! Leah also had a set of bad ass twins: a boy named Marmar and a girl name Juju. Cousin Deja loved them, but they were like little Tasmanian devils from the time they woke up until they went to sleep. In the three weeks that Deja had been there the twins had managed to break all 3 bottles of her Beyoncé perfumes, spill bleach on 2 pair of her House of Deréon jeans, and cut up a brand-new bundle of Brazilian body wave hair. This was not going to work with Deja. She had to move around as soon as possible. Deja was quickly growing tired of her surroundings.

Tamar Braxton's "Love and War" filled

the air. She started smiling. There was only one person that ringtone could belong to.

"Hey Omar." Deja said sultrily.

"What's good, Shorty?"

"Trying to keep my little cousins out of what's left of my clothes. What's up with you?"

"Shiiiid...Just pullin' up to my bro's crib bout to smoke. What chu doin' later?" he asked.

"Nothing. Why what's up?" she asked curiously.

"I have something romantic planned. I'ma scoop you up around 7."

Deja tried to keep her voice calm. "That's cool, Bae. I'll be ready. Bye." She hung up her phone. *Tonight. I will tell him tonight.* Deja thought to herself. They talked every single day since Omar rescued her from the middle of the street. She knew things were getting serious, and she was ready to take their relationship to a new level: a sexual level that she really wanted, and she was certain he wanted as well. Omar seemed like an open-minded guy. She didn't want this to be an episode of Jerry Springer, but she knew this is what she needed to do. Deja moved around her cousin's apartment getting herself ready for her date.

7 PM sharp. Omar arrived. Deja opened the door to see dark Timbaland boots, creased blue jeans, a green polo shirt, and a single herringbone gold chain around Omar's neck. His eyes dazzled behind his square eyeglasses that matched the color of his shirt. He was looking and smelling good. *Damn...do I have to wait until after the date?* Deja thought to herself as she hugged him. They didn't talk on the way to the restaurant. They didn't need to. He held her hand as they made their way across town to JMK Nippon's: a Japanese restaurant with tableside grills.

"Where's all the other people, O? This place is usually packed." Deja asked.

"Not tonight. Not for you." Omar responded.

"Wait. You rented this entire place? For us?" Deja asked.

"For you." Deja smiled. If he was really trying to impress her, it was working. The night continued just as heavenly as the beginning. They ate. They talked shit. They sipped wine. They made fun of the Korean chef's broken English. Deja softly bit her lip. Omar's eyes worked her body the entire night.

"Shorty, you know we been chillin' for about a month now and I'm feelin' you. So, I wonna take us to the next level." Deja immediately began to feel sick. The look of her discomfort started to appear on her face. "You ok?" Omar asked with concern.

"Yeah...I... I got somethin' to tell you" she replied nervously.

"Ok cool. Just let me get this off my chest first though." Omar took a deep breath. "We been chillin' for a lil' minute now. These past few weeks have been the happiest I've been in a long time, and I'm not tryna lose that. What I'm tryna say is...Shorty, I Love--"

"I was born a man!" Deja blurted out cutting Omar off.

"What?" Omar questioned in disbelief.

"I was born a man." Deja repeated timidly.

"Really? A man? That's the best you could

come up with? Bitch if you wasn't feelin' me like that, then all you had to say was you wasn't feelin' me like that! You ain't gotta lie! You like playin' games!!? You like fuckin' with a nigga's emotions?" Omar shouted as he stood up poundin' his fist on the table causing the wine to tip over.

"I'm not lyin'!" She shouted as she pushed away from the table in attempt not to let the now spilled wine run on to her brand-new skirt. "I WAS BORN A MAN! Why the fuck would I lie about somethin' like that, Omar?"

Omar looked around. He was not processing the news too well. If this was going to turn into that Jerry Springer episode, Deja was ready: skirt, heels, and all. Growing up in the hood as a young black gay boy, all she did was fight. She was no stranger to kicking some ass. Baby girl was lethal with the hands. Omar began to see the seriousness in her eyes and eased back down in his chair.

"So, you mean to tell me you have a dick?" he whispered.

"Yeah." she calmly replied. Omar jumped up, snatched Deja by the wrist, and yelled "LET'S GO!" He said nothing as he angrily stormed towards his SUV still holding on to

Deja's wrist. Once they made it to the truck Omar flung open her door and yelled "GET IN!" *This nigga trippin'.* She said to herself as he walked around and hopped in the truck slamming the door.

"What the fuck is wrong with you?" Deja screamed. "Don't be fuckin' snatchin' me up like that! Are you fuckin' crazy? I'll fuck you up--"

Omar dived on top of Deja, placed his hands around her throat, and began to kiss her passionately. Deja was in total shock, but she didn't resist. *What the fuck is goin' on?* she thought to herself. *Does he want me or is he going to kill me?* A million things ran through her mind as Omar started sucking on her neck while slowly sliding his hands up her dress. Deja instantly started to relax. The feeling of his masculine hands cuffing her now exposed breasts drove her wild. She let out a loud moan as he caressed and sucked on her nipples. They passionately hugged and kissed as they made their way to the back seat of Omar's truck. She couldn't believe this was happening! But why here and why now? She didn't want to lose her virginity this way, but it just felt so good and she loved every second of it. Omar continued to caress her body. He licked and sucked all over her thighs. Deja's body started to tremble. She was excited and nervous all at the same time. Omar slowly began to remove her panties, exposing her she-stick.

"STOP!" Deja yelled. Omar became confused.

"Somethin' wrong, Bae?" he replied.

"Don't you want this?"

"Yeah...believe me yeah...but there's something else I gotta tell you." She said out of breath.

"Ok. What's up Shorty?" He sat up in the back seat of his truck.

Deja sat up and bashfully looked him straight in the eyes.

"I'm a virgin."

CHAPTER 4

GIRL FIGHT

Walking through the fire
Please don't let me go
Take me to the river
I want you to knoooow
I'm burning up
Come put me out
Come and put me out

The sounds of Jessie J's "Burning Up" came blaring through the sound system while Deja was cleaning up her cousin's apartment. She finally cleaned Leah's pigsty of a residence. She even hired her own exterminator to come in and get rid of all the mice. After 2 ½ months of living there, she understood why the apartment was in such bad condition. Leah was an 18-year-old single mother who worked and went to school full-time. When she wasn't working or at school, she was pretty much trying to eat sleep or care for the twins. So, she never really had time to do her household duties. Deja stepped in and kept the house in tip top shape while her cousin was out handling business. Leah appreciated that.

"Leah! Hurry up Bitch! I gotta pee," Deja yelled annoyingly banging on the bathroom door.

Leah opened the door. "Girl, move! I'm late for work! Can you pick up the twins from daycare?" Leah rushed for the front door.

"Yeah." Deja shouted while rolling her eyes.

"Thanks, Cuz. I'll pick up some pizza for dinner." Leah quickly replied.

"OK Tuna!" Deja shot back.

Leah ran out the door slamming it behind her. Moments later there was a knock on the door.

"Bitch, did you forget your keys again?" Deja said playfully as she ran out the bathroom.

"Sup, Shorty?" Omar answered looking sexy as ever. Deja and Omar where still going strong. Their bond had become closer than ever after that night in the car. He explained that he had never been with a transsexual before. In a way, they were both virgins and agreed they would wait till the time was right. Together, they had become the hood's idolized power couple...like a ghetto version of Jay-Z and Beyoncé. Men wanted her and women hated her for having him. Deja didn't care. They knew better than to try her. She had already checked a few bitches out there.

"That's exactly what I came to talk to you about." Omar said while snatching her up by her waist and kissing her lustfully.

"What chu mean?" Deja asked curiously.

"You gone let me in?" Omar replied with a nasty grin on his face.

"Nah nigga." she said while biting her lip.

Omar picked Deja up and made his way into the apartment. She wrapped her legs around his waist and kissed him.

"What keys?" She said jumping off him and dancing her way back to the bathroom.

"You remember when I told you that my

cousin was moving to Cali?" Omar said while rambling through the fridge?

"Yeah." She yelled from the bathroom.

"Well, she got a 4 bedroom in Fairgrounds, and she not trying to give it up. So, I told her me and you would take it, and I would pay the rent while she was gone." he said while still rambling through the fridge.

"Are you serious?" Deja shouted in excitement as she flushed the toilet and ran into the living room.

"Yeah," he giggled. "These are your keys." he said dangling the keys in front of Deja's face.

"Oh my god. Oh My God! OH MY GOD!" Deja screeched as she tackled him onto the sofa.

"Omar, I Love You!" she shouted. Omar was stunned. He paused.

"I love you too, Shorty," he said kissing her lips. "I already had the crib fully furnished too."

"Really? It better be nice." Deja said

playfully. "So when can I move in?"

"Now! Go pack yo' shit, Shorty." Omar said while slapping' Deja on the ass.

Drake's lyrics blared through Omar's phone. "Aw shit, Shorty. I forgot I was supposed to make a run for my man's really quick." Omar said as he quickly headed for the door.

"It's cool Bae. I gotta go pick the twins up from daycare anyway." Deja responded.

Omar pecked her on the lips and darted out the door. "See you later Shorty!" He shouted before slamming the door. She smiled and danced around with her key and plopped on the sofa. *Fully furnished...wow. Wait...How was he...never mind.* She thought to herself.

Deja pulled up at Northwest Community Center Daycare to pick up the twins. She started feeling weird like somebody was watching her. Deja reached into her glove compartment and put her taser in her Louis Vuitton bag. She hopped out the car and looked around. Nothing. Maybe she was tripping. She shook it off and went inside.

"Welcome to the Northwest Community

Center. My name is Raheem. How may I be of assistance?"

Deja stood there in a daze. This man was so fine! She had never seen a man like him before. He was tall and slim like a chocolate version of Trey Songz without the braids. Deja didn't really like dark-skinned dudes, but she would make an exception.

"Uh...you okay?" he asked.

Deja was still sidetracked by how fine this man was. "Uhm yeah, I'm sorry," she chuckled. "I'm here to pick up my little cousins."

"Ok," he replied. "Just sign them out here and then walk through those double doors." he said as he handed her a clipboard. Deja signed the twins out, went and got them, then headed back to the crib. As soon as she opened the car door, Juju dashed into the building and Marmar was right behind her. Deja chased behind them. "Stop runnin'! Get y'all lil asses back here." she yelled. Deja got to the door and let the kids in the apartment.

"Excuse me. Are you Deja?" An unfamiliar female voice asked.

"Go in your room and play," she yelled to the twins while staying out in the hallway. Deja close the door.

"Yeah, I'm Deja. How may I help you?" she asked. This chick was high yellow and a bit on the chunky side. She had on a sundress with a lime green scarf on her head and what appeared to be a tattoo that said OMAR on the side of her face.

"I'm Kiara. Omar's ex," she said stepping a bit closer to Deja. "I just wanted to meet you in person and tell you that you need to move around. Omar and I are gettin' back together and we don't need yo' project ass in the way." Deja stood there rolling her eyes with her arms folded. *This bitch couldn't be serious,* she thought. Deja just stood and said nothing.

"Bitch, do you hear me?!," Kiara snapped. Still Deja didn't reply. "I knew you was a scary ass bitch. You got all these hoes out here scared to look at you, but I knew you wasn't bout that life!" Kiara said louder. The hallway instantly began to fill with people who wanted a front row seat to the drama that was quickly about to unfold.

"Just beat her ass, Kiki!" A voice yelled out from the crowd. Deja still said nothing.

"Bitch, you gone leave my man alone or I'ma beat yo' ass!" Kiara said as she pointed her finger in Deja's face. Deja could now see that Kiara wanted to put on a show. Deja was good at those.

"Bitch you done yet?" Deja asked. Kiara's eyes widened and punched Deja in the mouth.

"Watch yo' mouth bit--" POW! Before Kiara could finish her sentence, Deja was all over her ass like lightning in a snowstorm. Deja dragged Kiara out of the building. "Bitch is this what you wanted? You think shit sweet?" Deja kept repeating while kicking her in the face.

"Somebody get this bitch offa me!" Kiara screamed. Nobody moved. Deja continued to beat the shit out of Kiara and Kiara continued to scream. Omar scooped Deja up into the air carrying her into the house.

"LET ME THE FUCK GO! THAT BITCH HIT ME!" Deja kicked and screamed.

"Calm down!" Omar demanded.

"Fuck you Omar! Yo' Bitch hit me!" Deja snapped.

"That's not my bitch!" He shot back.

"Get the fuck out bitch ass nigga!" Deja screamed as she flung open the door. Omar slowly made his way out the door.

"Call me when you ain't--" BOOM! Deja slammed the door in his face. She couldn't believe this nigga had her out there fighting over him. *We done,* she said to herself. *I'm cool on his ass....*

CHAPTER 5

IRREPLACEABLE

Deja was furious. She couldn't believe Omar! *He's just like every other nigga,* she thought to herself. *I know that bitch is lying...right? Ugh! I can't believe I did that shit over him!* Deja's mind was racing a million miles a minute. She didn't know what to think at this point, and she needed answers. Just as she picked up her phone to call Omar, Leah bust through the front door.

"Bitch, what the fuck?!" Leah screamed.

"What?!" Deja confusingly replied.

"You got my kids, and you out here fightin' and shit! What the Fuck, Deja?!"

"Bitch yo' kids was in the house!" Deja snapped back.

"But I can still get evicted for that shit!" Leah replied.

"Look. She hit me, and ain't no bitch gone pop me and brag about it. So, fuck you and that eviction!" Deja shouted.

"Fuck me? You can pack yo' shit and get the fuck out with yo' fagget ass!" Leah screamed back. The room went silent for a moment.

"Fagget? Bitch, I got yo fagget! You my cousin and all but bitch you can get it too!" Deja said with a devilish grin.

Leah lowered her tone. "I'm sorry, cuz. I didn't mean that, but you know this is all I got. I got two kids to think about. I still love you, but you gotta go."

Deja took a deep breath. "I get it. I'll leave today." Deja packed her things and left. She went to the Quality Inn about 10 minutes away from Leah's house.

"Welcome to the Quality Inn. My name is Tuesday. How may I assist you?" He asked.

"Um, do you have any rooms available?" Deja asked.

To the Left to The Left... Beyoncé's "Irreplaceable" blasted through Deja's phone.

"Hold on love," Deja said to the hotel clerk.

"What?!" Deja snapped answering her phone.

"Where you at, Shorty?" Omar asked with concern.

"At the Quality Inn." Deja said drily.

"With who?!" Omar snapped.

"Nigga, don't you got a bitch?" Deja asked sarcastically.

"Yeah! You! The fuck?" he quickly responded.

"Can you meet me in Fairgrounds?"

"Fairgrounds?" Deja questioned.

"Can you meet me there or nah?!" Omar snapped.

"Yeah I can. I'll be there in 20 minutes. Text me the address" she replied. Then, she hung up.

"Honey thanks, but I guess I won't be needin' that room after all." Deja said giggling.

"It's cool, boo," Tuesday replied. "Did I here you say you're going to the FG's?"

This bitch was nosey as fuck, Deja thought to herself. "Yeah, "she replied.

"Well can I catch a ride with you? I get off in like 2 minutes, and it will be an hour before the next bus comes. I got gas money." Tuesday explained.

This bitch couldn't be serious, Deja thought. *I don't even know this ho.* "Oh, ok cool." Deja replied.

Tuesday smiled, "Thank you! Give me a second to punch out."

"I'll be in the car." Deja replied. Deja was very skeptical about giving this chick a ride. After getting to know each other on the way to Fairgrounds, he turned out to be cool.

Tuesday was about 5'9 with a very slim build. He was caramel complexion and was often mistaken as a female. His low-cut hair alone with his smooth baby face did him no justice as far as masculinity goes, and his soft feminine voice didn't help a bit either. He honestly looked like a girl trying to be a boy.

Deja had never really met another gay person or anyone close to being transgendered before. She felt like Tuesday would be her new best friend. They finally pulled up to the crib which just so happen to be right across the way from the address that Omar had sent.

"Do you wanna come in real quick while I get your gas money from my brother?" Tuesday asked.

"Sure," Deja replied.

"Raheem! Raheem!" Tuesday screamed when he walked in the house.

"What?!" Raheem shouted back walking into the kitchen with his shirt off.

Deja couldn't believe her eyes. *Twice in one day?* She said to herself. *This had to be some type of joke.*

"You got a 20?" Tuesday asked.

"Yeah," he replied annoyingly digging

into his pocket and handing the $20 to Tuesday while focusing on Deja. "How you doin' Ma?" he said seductively.

"I'm good." Deja replied flirtatiously.

Deja's phone rang. It was Omar. She ignored the call. "He can definitely wait." she said aloud.

"Damn Ma. You do yo' mans like that?" Raheem asked sarcastically.

"Yeah. He gettin' back with his ex so... it is what it is." She responded.

"Shidd...well in that case drop that zero and get you a hero!" Raheem said while attempting to flex his chest and abs.

"I just might have to." Deja replied.

"Ahem," Tuesday cleared his throat.

"Here girl," he said handing Deja the $20.

"Thanks for the ride! Let me walk you out." Tuesday said pushing Deja towards the door.

"Nah bruh. I'll walk her out. Take yo' ol'

hatin' ass upstairs," Raheem snapped.

Tuesday sucked his teeth and went upstairs.

"So, can I get yo' number?" Raheem asked.

"Damn! You get right to the point, don't you?," Deja replied. "I can't give you my number, but I can take yours."

Raheem smiled. His pretty white teeth glistened in the sunlight. She put his number in her phone and headed for the door. Her phone rang again, and she ignored the call.

"Damn Ma, you just gone leave without sayin' bye?" Raheem asked.

"My bad," Deja replied. She turned around and gave him a hug. She squeezed his neck tight and kissed him on the cheek. Y*eah...he wants it*, Deja thought to herself. Deja headed back to her car.

"So, that's what we do now?" Omar asked stopping Deja right in her tracks.

CHAPTER 6

DRUNKIN LOVE

Deja stood there looking like she had seen a ghost. She honestly didn't know what to say.

"So that's what we do now? We ignorin' each other's phone calls?" Omar asked again.

Deja immediately relaxed. Omar hadn't seen her hug and kiss Raheem. So, she played it off.

"Tuesday was using my phone," she replied.

"Man, don't play games with me! If you wanna end this shit, then end it!" Omar snapped. He clearly had been drinking.

"Did I say I wanted to end it?" she softly asked.

"So why the fuck you ignorin' my calls then?" he barked.

"I told you," Deja said sternly, "Tuesday was using my phone! What's wrong with you?"

"Bitch, don't give me that bullshit!" He shouted.

Deja slapped the slob from his mouth. "Who you callin' a bitch? You betta watch yo' fuckin mouth Omar!" she snapped. Omar chuckled and grabbed Deja by her arm and pulled her closer to him.

"You so fuckin crazy! Gimme a kiss!" he said as he leaned in puckering his lips.

"Omar, stop it! You're drunk. You hurtin' my arm, and you're making a fuckin' scene." Deja said snatching away and heading for her car. She loved Omar, but she wasn't going to be embarrassed by him or anybody for that matter. This was not her cup of tea.

"Shorty...where you goin'?" he drunkenly shouted.

"The hell away from you!" Deja screamed. Omar chased behind her. "Come in the crib. I gotta show you somethin'!"

Deja kept walking. "Shorty! Shorty wait! DEJA!" He yelled out.

"What Omar?!" She yelled back while opening her car door.

"Would you fuckin' stop!" Omar shouted while slamming her door shut.

"Nigga you got me Fu--" Omar cut her off by lustfully kissing her.

She pushed him away slapping him again. "Stop it!" She yelled.

Omar kissed her again. "Shorty, they watchin' us. Now calm down." He whispered aggressively while pulling her closer to him. Deja could feel his manhood growing hard against her stomach. Now she was turned on.

"Who's watchin'?" she asked. Deja turned to see that everybody was outside watching them. Even Raheem and Tuesday were out there, at 2 AM, watching the hood soap opera unfold.

"Can we take this inside?" Deja seductively asked. Omar scooped Deja up and carried her toward the crib.

"I got somethin' to show you" he said as he used one hand to unlock the door.

"What is it?" she asked quietly.

"Welcome home, Shorty. Your queendom awaits you." Omar said as he closed the door and placed her on her feet. Deja turned around and couldn't believe her eyes. This apartment was amazing. Everything was purple, black and silver. Even the kitchen appliances. Every room had a 72-inch flat-screen TV, and all the furniture was customized. The living room and dining room were filled with big purple life like artificial flowers, statues, and a myriad of paintings. He had turned one room into a fitness center, another into a game spot, another into a guest room and the biggest room was the master bedroom. The basement was furnished with purple plush carpet and decked out with a bar and lounge area. He even built a little laundry room down there.

"So, what you think?" he asked. Deja didn't say a word she just walked through the house admiring everything. She was speechless. *I don't deserve this. Fuck! Why did I kiss Raheem? And how did Omar get this stuff? This...this is too much*, Deja thought to herself.

"We need to talk" she blurted out.

CHAPTER 7

21 QUESTIONS

"What did I do wrong now?" He asked confused.

"Start with Kiara. Explain. Now." Deja replied with a serious look and her arms crossed like she was his momma or something.

"Really?" Omar chuckled. "Man, Shorty check this, if I wanted that Bitch then she would be here not you. That's my past, and I promise you, ain't no future in that. Unless she gets on some more bullshit and you gotta beat that ass once again," Omar laughed. "Oh my god Shorty, you beat the fuck outta her! I watched that shit for a good little minute and was like 'Damn, my Shorty got hands!' I mean you ain't got shit on me doe," he bragged. "But, shidd I'ma have to test those out to see if you can throw 'em with the fellas." Omar said as he playfully jabbed at Deja.

"I'm not done, and I don't see shit funny Omar," Deja snapped.

"OK OK Shorty, my bad. What's up?" Omar said attentively.

"Why are you doing all this?" Deja asked.

"Doing what?" He shot back.

"This!" Deja replied as she looked around the room.

"What are you really trying to ask? You not makin' sense" Omar responded.

"What I'm askin' is why you buying me all these nice things? What's your motive behind it? Do you really love me like you say you do or are you just trying to take my virginity?"

"Are you fuckin' serious? You think I did all this shit just to get some ass?! I did this shit cuz I want the best for you. That's what real niggas do!" He shouted while beating on his chest! "They look out for the ones they love expectin' nothing in return. Man, I wanna be yo' first, but I'm not gone buy yo' virginity. That's somethin' money can't buy!"

Deja's face softened as her heart melted. "You're serious?" She asked.

"Yes." He said calmly.

"I feel you on all that and I'm so grateful for everything that you have done for me, but I've never been with someone like you. This just seems a little too good to be true. Guys like you don't usually stick around too long, especially with girls like me," she explained.

"I'm not the average guy!" Omar angrily replied.

Deja walked over to Omar and gently kissed him. "I love you too," she said as she wrapped her arms around the back of his neck. Omar grabbed her waist then quickly began to caress her lower back and soft ass. He scooped Deja up and carried her up to their room.

Gently lying her on their brand-new California king sized bed, he began to kiss her passionately. He snatched his shirt off, climbed on top of Deja, and exposed her breasts. He admired them for a second. Omar sucked and licked all over them, and Deja didn't resist. She loved the feeling of his strong hands all over her body. It made her feel like a real woman. She began to moan.

Omar slid off her pants, flipped her over, and started eating her ass like groceries. He licked and sucked on Deja's hole like it was his last meal. Deja was in heaven, it felt so good that she started running up the bed. He grabbed her by the waist, lifted her ass straight in the air, and continued to eat. Deja balanced herself in a handstand. She could now see Omar's rock-hard print throbbing through his pants. She pulled out his thick swollen meat stick and took all of him into her mouth.

"Shiiid...damn girl." Omar moaned quietly. He released her thighs allowing her to fall into a back-bend position. Without removing Omar from her throat, she spun around onto her hands and knees and went to work.

"FFFFuck Shorty!," Omar blurted out. "You betta stop or I'ma fuck around and cum!" Deja's mouth got even wetter. She sucked him harder and faster. He grabbed Deja's hair and began forcing his rock-hard pulsating manhood down her throat. This is exactly what Deja was waiting for. As he forcefully plowed her face, she sucked even harder.

"Oh shit," Omar grunted, "I'm finna cum!" She didn't stop. She let every drop of his warm creamy load slide right down her throat. Omar was speechless. He laid down on the bed. Deja hopped up and headed towards the bathroom.

"Bae," she called out.

"What's up Shorty?" Omar faintly responded.

"Can I ask you one more question?" she asked.

"Anything." he replied while sitting up.

"What are you gonna do if the hood finds out my secret?"

CHAPTER 8

PARTY

"Open up the doe f'ore I knock it down Hoe!" Tuesday chanted as he banged on Deja's Door.

"Bitch I'm comin'!" Deja yelled as she quickly snatched open the door.

"Bitch you wasn't comin' fast enough! You know how big this dam box is?" Tuesday asked.

"Well now whose fault is that?" Deja playfully snapped.

"It's this Bitch's fault. Now move! This shit is heavy!" Tuesday playfully shot back in his Monique from *Precious* voice. He plopped the box on the kitchen counter.

"Girl what the hell is this?" Deja asked.

"This, my friend, is what we call do it 'fluids'!" Tuesday replied opening the box and exposing all the different varieties of alcohol.

"Yessss gawd honey!" Deja answered as she began to playfully twerk while still wrapped in a towel. It had been three weeks since Omar had moved her into her new crib, and two days since he had been out of town on business. Deja had begun to feel lonely and bored. A house party seemed like the perfect way for her to gain some excitement and finally let her hair down. Deja had never drank before. With Omar gone, there was no one to stop her tonight.

"Where the fuck are yo' clothes?" Tuesday interrupted.

"Upstairs My shower was rudely interrupted by somebody and they damn do it 'fluid'." Deja sarcastically responded.

"Well get yo' ass back upstairs and hop to it! People will start arriving shortly."

"Do you think people really gone show up?" Deja asked.

"Bitch, you can get black people to show up anywhere with three things: free food, free liquor, and loud music. " Tuesday answered.

"Hell, not only will they show up, but they gone be on time." They both paused for a moment then laughed in unison.

"Alright then bitch! Let me finish getting' cute!" Deja said breaking the laughter.

"I'ma bring over the food and then I'ma run back to the crib and change." Tuesday replied. Deja ran up the stairs and Tuesday ran back out the door.

In just a few hours, Tuesday had set up the food, situated the bar, got the DJ and his equipment in place, and still managed to get dressed before the guests began to arrive. Meanwhile, Deja was still upstairs deciding on what to wear.

"Bitch, what is taking you so long? It's almost 10:30!" Tuesday yelled as he busted into Deja's room without warning. He was wearing some white, grey and blue Nikes, black jeans and an Orlando Magic's Jersey that said McGrady with the number 1 on the back. Deja stood in the closet doorway in distress. She was bare foot wearing a red, black and white Dennis Rodman Chicago Bulls Jersey dress. Her hair was bone strait and hung just below her breast.

"Bitch I'm tryna decide on what shoes to wear," she whined. "Should I wear my Louboutin's or my red and black 13s?" Deja continued as she held up both pairs of shoes for Tuesday to see.

"Bitch, this is a house party, not a dinner party," Tuesday started, "You can put them heels on tryna be cute around these hood rats if you want to, and you liable to get yo' ass beat in yo' own house. If you stay ready you ain't gotta get ready! Now put them J's on and bring yo' ass!" Tuesday said before leaving and slamming the bedroom door.

The moment the DJ started playing music people began to arrive just as Tuesday predicted. The party quickly filled with all sorts of people. Some Deja knew or she had seen before around the hood. Those who she didn't know all knew who she was. *Tuesday really out done himself,* Deja thought to herself.

Deja and Tuesday were both standing in the kitchen getting ready to take shot number 6 of Hennessy. The shot glass liquid hit her lips but spilled on her dress. Deja turned around to address the person responsible. She came face to face with a female who could have been a linebacker for somebody's NFL team. She was dark skinned and wore some black flats, with metallic leggings and a dingy white tee. She had about 4 to 5 inches of hair that was slicked down in the front and stood straight up in the back like a ghetto Tina Turner. Two light skinned shorter versions of her who appeared to be twins stood on the left and right side behind her. All three women looked like they had just rolled out of bed and came to the party, especially the biggest one. You could still see the sleep in the corners of her eyes.

"Excuse you," the female said to Deja.

"No, Bitch. Excuse YOU." Tuesday aggressively chimed in before Deja could speak.

"Who you callin' a bitch?!" One of the twins snapped.

"I'm talking to this manly ass Bitch!" Tuesday shouted as he pointed his finger in the biggest one's face.

"It's ok Toot. We gone give the Gross Sisters a pass tonight. We not on that." Deja replied in attempt to calm Tuesday down.

"Gross Sisters?!" The three women shrieked in unison. Without hesitation, the biggest one reached out to grab Deja only for it to be quickly blocked by Raheem. He liked watching her enjoy this beautiful night, but with this drama about to quickly unfold, Deja's beautiful night was easily about to turn in to a blood bath.

"Ladies, and Gentle-MAN, this is not what we came out for," Raheem shouted over the blaring music while eyeing all of them. "If you are not here to have a good time, then GO THE FUCK HOME." he continued while slightly lifting his shirt and revealing a pistol to the three women. The women headed for the door. Shortly after, Raheem leaned over and whispered to Deja, "Can I holla at you for a sec?"

"Nah nigga. She got a man." Tuesday butted in.

"Nigga, stop hatin'!" Raheem shot back while grabbing Deja's hand and leading her outside.

"Where are you taking me?" Deja asked.

"Damn Ma! I can't talk to you for a sec?" Raheem said with a smirk.

"You on some other shit, and I can't be leavin' all those people in my crib like that." Deja replied.

"Man Tuesday in there. I just wanted to chill with you alone for a quick sec." he shot back. Raheem's phone began to ring.

"Fuck!" he shouted as he looked down at his phone. "Aye Ma. I gotta make a run real quick! Go back inside. I'll be back before the party over." Raheem said as he quickly released Deja's hand jumped in his car and sped off.

"Bitch did you think this shit was over?!" a familiar voice said from behind. Deja turned around. Kiara and the Gross Sisters were back in her face. Deja knew how this would end, but she wasn't gonna show any fear.

"Actually I did...seeing as Omar had to pull me up off of you the last time we met." She continued.

"Well Omar ain't here to pull you off me now! So, what's up?!" Kiara replied with a smirk.

"Run up!" Deja taunted. She figured this wasn't gonna be a fair fight. When she noticed the smaller two Gross Sisters attempting to close her in to a circle, Deja immediately began to take steps back in search of a wall. She knew she did not stand a chance with these four big women if they surrounded her. She had to somehow gain some type of leverage, but it was too late.

Kiara threw the first punch causing Deja to stumble into the biggest sister, who immediately fired off with the second punch. The other two sisters joined in and began attacking Deja like lions on a gazelle. Deja tried her best to rumble with the four women, but she was no match for them all. She was throwing some good blows, but it wasn't phasing Kiara and the Sisters.

"Bitch where's Omar Now?!" They were all pulling hair and pounding on her at the same time screaming.

Tuesday's attention was swiftly caught by the Gross Sisters and another fat light skinned chick pummeling some girl in red. Tuesday took a few steps closer and began to guzzle the Hennessy he had left in the bottle. Then he caught a glimpse of the Rodman 91 jersey. Tuesday immediately began to smile as he realized it was Deja in the center getting knocked around like a pinball.

"You Bitches had to jump me!" Deja screamed as she rapidly fired off unphased blows. She was trying with all her might to get the four women to back off, but they wouldn't let up. Deja felt herself becoming tired. She rushed Kiara to the ground and commenced pounding her in the face. Meanwhile, the sisters began to kick and punch her in the head.

"Get this bitch off of me!" Kiara shouted.

The commotion from the fight now caused everyone in the party to curiously come outside. Immediately noticing the audience, Tuesday sprang into action. "NOT MY BEST FRIEND," he yelled while clocking the sisters with the Hennessy bottle.. The sisters began to retreat leaving Kiara to be finished off alone.

"Bitch...The...Very...Next...Time...You... Come... Near... Me... I'ma... Kill... You!" Tears began to roll down Deja's cheeks as she sat on Kiara pounding her in the face screaming. Kiara was no longer putting up a fight as Tuesday began to pull Deja off her. Deja didn't resist. She was exhausted.

"Come on, best friend. She got the point." He said. Deja sluggishly made her way through the crowd and to the crib with the help of Tuesday.

"Party Over! Everybody GET THE FUCK OUT!" Deja screamed.

CHAPTER 9

WHAT AM I GONNA DO?

I was excited
Cause I was fallin'
Fallin' in love with you
Now that I've fallen
What am I gonna do...

The sounds of Tyrese blared through the speakers of Deja's Ford Focus as she and Tuesday headed west down E State Street. They had just finished doing some retail therapy at Cherryvale Mall, and now they were making their way back to the projects. Deja and Tuesday had gotten even closer since the party. Tuesday had proven his 'loyalty' to Deja, and she felt like she was in his debt. If you saw one, you saw the other (unless they were with their men).

"Ah Biiiiiiitch." Tuesday giggled while scrolling through his phone.

"Girl what?" Deja asked.

"Tell me why Kiara made Omar her Man Crush Monday on Facebook?" Tuesday said showing her his phone.

"See? That Bitch pickin'." Deja replied rolling her eyes.

"I didn't say nothing to you about it, but I saw that bitch in the food court. I know she seen me, cuz she started doin' the most. I guess she felt unfuckwithable since she was with her fat dirty ass sisters." Tuesday answered.

Deja laughed. "But I bet that bitch didn't want a round three doe!"

Tuesday chimed in. "Cuz if you swing, I swing. Okaay?"

They high fived! "Ooh girl. Stop at this gas station so I can get me some cigarettes." Tuesday demanded.

"Bitch, why you didn't get cigarettes at the corner store in the mall?" Deja asked.

"Because they high as fuck in the mall," Tuesday shot back sarcastically.

"Here. Put 20 on pump 2." She said handing Tuesday the money.

"You lucky I love you." Tuesday replied as he got out the car.

"You lucky I stopped!" Deja shot back.

Tuesday walked into the station and stood in line. It was packed as usual, and the Arab man had to talk shit to everybody who came up to the window.

"Can y'all hurry the Fuck up?! I got somewhere to be!" A voice yelled from behind. Tuesday turned around.

"Just when you thought it was safe for a bitch to go outside!" he shouted as he greeted his ex-boyfriend Justin.

"Uh...hey bae." Justin said in shock.

"Bitch don't gimme that shit," Tuesday snapped, "You stole my car and fucked it up! You owe me 27 stacks and I want my coins now!"

"You'll never get it," Justin shot back jokingly.

Tuesday punched Justin in the face. He stumbled back out of the gas station door.

"You crazy bitch!" Justin screamed with blood gushing from his nose into his mouth.

"Bitch you think I was gone let you get away with that?! You shoulda prayed they gave you life, cuz now you finna lose it bitch." Tuesday blasted.

Justin turned around and attempted to run, but Tuesday snatched him by his mohawk and slammed him to the ground. Justin jumped right back up.

"You wanna fight?" Justin said spitting blood from his mouth. Tuesday ran up swinging. They went blow for blow but after a few hard blows to the face Justin was no match for Tuesday. Tuesday slammed Justin on the ground and quickly hopped on top of him.

"I told you bitch, I told you! Where's my money," Tuesday screamed while punching him repeatedly. *Damn Tuesday got hands! I think he got this one.* Deja thought as she watched the action from her car. Deja spotted some tall ass Sheryl Underwood lookin' bitch push her way through the crowd screaming

"Not my brother!" and kicked Tuesday in the face causing Justin to jump on top of him. Within seconds, Deja was out of the car and on her ass.

"Bitch, you got my bestie fucked up!" Deja spat. Deja snatched up this chick and drug her by her hair like she was a rag doll. This girl was twice the size of Deja in weight, and she was swinging slow and hard. Deja knew if one of those punches landed it was over for her, but she wasn't going to give her the opportunity to do that. Deja ran circles around the tall amazon woman, but she caught Deja in the side of her head causing Deja to stumble and almost fall. Without thinking, Deja picked up a Snapple bottle and busted her in the face shattering glass everywhere.

"Biiiiiiitch! I'ma fuck you up!" The big woman screamed in rage with blood pouring out of her forehead. "This shit ain't over Bitch, and you betta believe that!" She roared as she sped off.

Deja and Tuesday jumped back in the car and head back to the crib. "What the fuck was that shit about?!" Deja asked.

"Girl, I been waitin to catch that bitch for almost a year now! He the reason I'm catchin' the bus to and from work. We dated for about two years, right? Then, that fucker stole my brand-new car, went to another bitch house to fuck, and then crashed it! He went to jail for it, but I still want my damn coins!" Tuesday explained.

Deja began to simmer down a bit. "Ohhhhh. I don't blame you. I woulda tapped that ass too. And you was workin' that hoe until Sasquatch jumped in." Deja replied.

"That Bitch couldn't take me," Tuesday replied giggling, "Thanks for havin' my back too by the way."

"Didn't you say earlier 'If you swing, I swing'? And besides, I owed you one," Deja said as they pulled up to the projects.

Tuesday gasped. "Oh my god. Best friend look!" Tuesday pointed.

"What the police out here for now?" Deja sarcastically asked as she parked her car.

"Deja! Deja! It's Omar!" Dominic frantically screamed as he ran up to the car. "They just ran up and cuffed him! We been calling you for the last 30 minutes!"

Deja looked down at her phone. It was dead.

"Where is Omar now?" She asked nervously.

"He's over there in the squad car." Dominic said. Deja headed towards the car and was greeted by this tall, bald headed, dark skinned officer.

"You need somethin'?" he asked.

"Yeah," Deja quickly shot back, "I need to speak to Omar. He got my key to the house," she lied.

"You got 2 minutes," the officer said opening Omar's door.

"Bae what's goin' on?" Deja asked in a desperate tone.

"Man Shorty, it's too much to explain right now. Just know I might be gone for a while." He said.

"What?" Deja cried.

"You good Shorty. Don't trip." He giggled.

"I'll call you when I'm downtown." He kissed Deja and got back in the car. Deja was confused. *Why isn't he taking this seriously? What the fuck was he laughing for? What did he do? Why wouldn't he tell me? What did he mean by I was good?* A million things raced through her mind. Deja's heart dropped. Omar was her everything, and he knew that.

"What am I gonna do now?" Deja cried as she made her way to the crib.

CHAPTER 10

COLLECT CALL

Deja stood up and walked out of the visiting room without saying goodbye. She had enough. It had been 3 weeks since Omar had gotten himself locked up, and this was already beginning to take a toll on her emotionally. Omar made sure Deja had any and everything she wanted and needed while he was away, but the reason that he was in jail in the first place was ludicrous.

Will you except my collect call?
Will you accept my collect call?

TI blared from Deja's phone as it rang. "Hello?" She answered.

"This is the Winnebago County Correctional Facility. You have a collect call from 'Omar'. To accept, press one." Deja accepted the call.

"Hello! Hello! Shorty, why the fuck you leave like that for?!" Omar snapped.

"I told you, Omar. I can't take this shit no more. This shit is all new to me. The fact that you held the shit from me for so long pisses me off! I mean I understand this is your life and all, but you could have at least given me the opportunity to choose whether or not I wanted to be a part of somethin' like this." Deja cried.

"Why we gotta talk about this shit on every visit and every phone call?" he asked.

"Because I feel played! I was real about everything from day one and you hid the fact that you was sellin' dope from me for months! Why?"

"Shorty, I did this shit for you tho. I just want the best for you. Man, I wasn't doin' none of this shit before I met you, but all you can do is bitch! You an ungrateful ass mothafucka!" he replied.

"Ungrateful? I've never asked you for shit Omar! You did all that shit on your own. At what point did I make you feel like you had to go and sell dope?" Deja felt herself getting ready to cry as she spoke, "Why didn't you just talk to me? You assumed I needed all those things, but my bank account was on fleek before I met you! I don't need shit from you Omar!" That was it. The tears started pouring. She continued. "Omar, I chose you because you was a compliment to me not because you could upgrade me!"

"Shorty....I... I'm sorry. I was just tryna make you happy," Omar pleaded. "I promise I didn't know it would turn out like this. Give me some time. I'll fix this I'll be home soon. Don't trip."

"And I guess I'm supposed to be happy while you on lock down, huh?" Deja asked sarcastically.

"Well," Omar replied. "I mean I want you to do this bid with me, but also I want you to live yo' life too. Shorty, I think we should take a break until I come home."

"What?!" Deja said confused.

"Man, I made some fucked up choices, and I need to deal with them. It's not fair for me to ask you to put your life on hold for me while I do this time and honestly, I don't expect you to."

"So you breakin' up with me?" Deja said with dismay.

"Nah Shorty... I still want visits, letters, and phone calls. I just don't want you to feel obligated to be with me while I'm in here. I don't want you to worry about me. I want you to enjoy life while I'm gone. And guess what? I'm all yours once I'm home. I just don't want to hurt you like this while I'm locked up." Omar said softly.

"But you're hurtin' me now" she snapped back.

"Man Shorty...." Omar started.

You have one-minute remaining for this call. The operator interrupted.

"Shorty, I love you and I'll call you tomorrow."

"I love you too bae," Deja replied. She put the phone down as her heart tore into pieces. Time would heal her eventually, but it wasn't going to start that process today. She glanced up at the jailhouse playing Omar's words over and over in her head. *Enjoy life while I'm gone. Don't feel obligated to me. How can I do without you?* She thought to herself. She wiped her face and silenced her sniffles. *I...I can't deal with this right now. I need...help. Tuesday. Tuesday can help.* She peeled out of the jailhouse parking lot heading to the FG's.

Deja banged on Tuesday's door like she was the police. "Toot! It's me! Open up!" She cried. The door opened to reveal a beautiful brown skin body with water droplets glistening down his chest.

"Raheem?" Deja said shocked.

CHAPTER 11

TEMPTATION

"Do I look like Toot to you?" Raheem asked.

"Actually...you do." Deja replied as she pushed her way into the house.

"Man, you got jokes, we don't look shit alike," Raheem chuckled, "Tuesday ain't never been this sexy, and besides that nigga is my stepbrother."

Stepbrother? Tuesday acts like they ass came out the same coochie. Deja thought to herself.

"Boy bye, where my best friend at?" Deja said rolling her eyes.

"Shidd...I don't know. Probably somewhere being a thot with his man or whatever he calls him." Raheem jokingly replied.

"Boy, you got my bestie fucked up," she shot back. "But anyway...tell him I stopped by," Deja said as she headed for the door.

"Wait," Raheem said as he grabbed Deja's hand. "Why you in a rush to leave so soon?"

Deja could see where this was headed and clearly it was no place good. "Boy, let me go," she said still pulling on the doorknob. "This ain't that, and I got somewhere to be! Just tell Tuesday I came b--"

Raheem's lips met Deja's mouth. Her whole body melted for a couple of seconds. Then, she remembered...Omar. Deja used as much strength as she had and pushed Raheem away. His towel dropped to the floor.

"Boy St... Oh. My Damn." Deja stared at Raheem's throbbing and hard dick.

"What? See something you like?" Raheem asked.

"Well...I...uh...I mean...shit....I...uh...you know...I...uh... you know I can't do this Raheem... cuz of...um...shit! What's that nigga name?" Deja asked out loud to herself.

"Man stop actin' like you don't want it. I

see the way you be lookin' at me. Yo' mouth sayin' no but yo' body sayin' yes." he said seductively.

He ain't wrong, Deja said to herself.

"Come 'ere." Raheem whispered as he gently pulled Deja closer to his completely naked body. Deja shook her head no, but she didn't resist.

"Man, why you actin all scared for," he asked.

"Cuz, this ain't what you lookin' for." she replied.

"What you mean?" Raheem asked.

Deja gently flicked his dick then whispered in his ear, "I'm just like you."

Raheem rolled his eyes and sucked his teeth. "Man get off that bullshit. I already know what it is." Deja quickly became delighted and shocked all at the same time. Other than when her brothers did it, her tea had never been clocked before.

"How did you know?" she asked curiously.

"Man, my bro was on some hatin' shit and told me everything. I guess he thought that would turn me off or somethin'" he replied.

That late ass bitch. Why he telling my business like that? Deja thought to herself.

"So, what's up Ma?," He asked as he placed her hand on his long fat semi hard dick. "Is you finna take dis dick or nah?"

"It's whateva" she replied.

Raheem started sucking her neck and squeezing her ass. Raheem slowly walked her to the living room and laid her on the couch. He kissed her passionately and started to unbutton her pants. Deja didn't stop him. She didn't even flinch. She just laid there enjoying the attention.

Raheem stopped and admired her body. He licked and sucked her nipples and rubbed all over her stick. Deja was loving it. Raheem seemed to know exactly what to do with every part of her body. He slowly and seductively placed her girl-wood in his mouth. Raheem sucked and slurped all over Deja's meat until she was about to cum. Then he stopped. He flipped Deja over on all fours and started to eat her ass like it was his last meal.

Deja couldn't believe this boy was dominating her like this, but she damn sure liked it. *Raheem is a pro!* she thought to herself. If he wanted to go any further, she was ready and willing to go the distance.

"You ready to take this dick Ma?" he asked in a low sexy tone?

"Yesssss...." Deja responded quietly. Her mouth was saying yes, her body was saying yes, but, on the inside, Deja was screaming no. She was nervous as hell, but she had to play it cool. Raheem spit in his hand, rubbed it all over his massive dick and slowly began to insert it into her tight virgin hole. *Oh shiiiit...* Deja thought. Deja felt the worst pain she had ever felt in her life. She felt like this boy had razor blades on the tip of his dick. Deja let out a painful moan. Raheem stopped.

"You ok, Ma?" he asked.

She clearly wasn't, but she didn't want to appear scared. Deja wanted to be known as a beast when it came to her sex game.

"Yeah" she replied. He pulled out and applied more saliva to his dick.

"Relax Ma" he said in a whisper tone. He

gently began to massage her hole with his dick and within a few seconds Deja began to receive him. At first, she was still a little uncomfortable but after a few slow strokes, Raheem started to feel good inside her. Deja let out a moan which was like a green light to Raheem because he started to speed up. Deja was so warm and tight.

After about 2 minutes, he knew that at that speed he wasn't gone last too long inside her. Raheem wanted to savor this moment, so he began to slow down but like clockwork Deja started throwing that ass back at him. She wanted to be fucked, and she wanted to be fucked hard.

"Hit this ass, Nigga!" Deja moaned. She was in heaven. If she had known sex was fire like this, she would have done it sooner. Deja was ready to show out now. So, she started throwing her ass back harder and faster.

"Aw Shhhitt!" Raheem moaned as he grabbed Deja by her 22-inch Brazilian hair and began to rapidly penetrate her deeply.

"Oh my god!" she screamed with pleasure.

"Aw shit! Take dat dick!" Raheem grunted back while smacking her ass. Deja's body began to tremble as she had never experienced this type of pleasure before. Raheem hammered in and out of Deja's pulsating hole. Deja started to jack herself off.

"I'm about to cum! I'm bout to cum!" She shouted. They both moaned and groaned so loudly that they didn't hear the door open.

"What the fuck?!" Tuesday shouted.

CHAPTER 12

CAUGHT UP

"So, you gay now?!" Tuesday asked directing all her attention to Raheem. Raheem jumped up and attempted to cover himself with a pillow.

"Man Joe, gone wit' all dat bullshit," Raheem shouted. Deja started to laugh as she put back on her clothes. After seeing Tuesday's reaction, she knew that they were much more than stepbrothers.

"Bitch what the fuck you laughing at? Get the fuck outta my house!" Tuesday shouted at Deja. Deja continued to get dressed slowly. "Bitch you think this a joke?!" Tuesday continued lividly.

"Bitch I'm not studin' you," Deja calmly replied. Tuesday dived for Deja, but Raheem caught him midair. "Man gone upstairs with that bullshit." Raheem shouted while holding on to Tuesday.

"Get off me 'Heem! You fuckin' this dude in my house!" Tuesday said snatching away.

"You act like you fuckin' him or somethin'." Deja said plainly. Tuesday became silent.

"Man, take yo' ass upstairs!" Raheem demanded once again. Tuesday huffed and puffed then stomped upstairs like a mad 5-year-old.

"Stay the fuck away from my brother you fuckin' he-she," Tuesday shouted as he stomped up the stairs.

"Keyword BROTHER," Deja shouted back. "What the fuck is his problem," she said now gaining Raheem's attention.

"Man, I don't know! He probably needs some **DICK**," Raheem shouted emphasizing on the word dick.

"Y'all fuckin' around or something?" Deja asked.

"Nah," Raheem explained. "We just did a little somethin' as kids and mothafuckas just can't seem to let that shit go."

Deja knew that a little too well. She herself use to hunch on her cousins when they were little, but that was like 12 years ago. It was harmless kid stuff now. It wasn't anything too serious to the point where she was ready to fight their now grown girlfriends and wives. Tuesday had issues and Deja wanted nothing to do with them.

"Well, I guess I should get going." Deja said with a grin.

"Nah Ma. Spend the night with me." Raheem begged.

Was this nigga crazy? she thought to herself. "I'm good," Deja started, "Besides, I would hate to have to fuck yo' bitch ass BROTHER up." she said referring to Tuesday.

"Ok. So, when am I gone see you again?" Raheem asked.

"I don't know. I'll text you." Deja said. They hugged, kissed, and Deja went home.

***

Five months passed and Deja sat in her room contemplating what she should do. Omar was being released today, and she still hadn't broken things off with Raheem yet. Since they slept together, Raheem had fallen deeply in love. Deja wasn't really feeling Raheem like that. He was a sweetheart. He had amazing potential as a boyfriend, but it was more about the sex for her. He had good head, good dick, and good ass. It just wasn't enough. Deja was in love with Omar. She planned on being with him once he was released. She kept in contact with Omar through his whole 6-month bid and even explained to him that she was seeing Raheem. Omar told her he understood, and he appreciated that she kept things 100 with him. Deja knew Raheem had feelings for her, but she didn't know how strong they were.

I guess I'ma have to let him down easy, she said to herself. Deja picked up her phone and called Raheem.

"What's up sexy?" Raheem said answering the phone.

"Boy stop," Deja giggled. "What you doin'?"

"Shit...at the crib smoking," he answered.

"Well we need to talk really quick. Can you come over?" Deja said nervously.

"Yeah bae. Is everything ok?" Raheem asked with concern.

"Yeah," Deja answered, "We just need to talk that's all."

It wasn't long before Deja heard a knock on her front door.

"Hey Bae--" Deja was interrupted by Raheem's lips and strong arms around her body. Deja forgot why she asked him to come over. Raheem guided her upstairs to the bedroom. When her leg touched the end of her bed, she remembered why he was here.

"Raheem stop" she moaned. Raheem paid her request no mind. "Raheem. Stop!" She said louder. He continued to suck on her neck and ear. "RAHEEM STOP!" She yelled while pushing him off.

"Damn Bae! What's wrong?" he asked with a confused look on his face.

"I said I wanted to talk." Deja responded.

"Well why you didn't just say that shit

then?"

"I said it on the phone."

"My bad, Ma. You know how I get when I'm near that body." He said slapping her ass. "So, what you wanna talk about?"

A knock on the door interrupted her explanation. Deja headed downstairs and Raheem followed.

"Who is it?" she yelled. There was no answer. "I said...who is it?" She yelled again this time snatching the door open.

"Is that how you greet the man of the house?" Omar said holding a big ass teddy bear and some red roses!

CHAPTER 13

TORN

Deja stood there. No words. No voice. She didn't have the slightest clue on how to address this situation. Even though she could see the look of hurt and disappointment written all over Raheem's face, she couldn't find the words to fix it. Hurting Raheem was never her intentions, but the cat was out of the bag now. There was nothing she could do to hide it. As the three of them stood looking at one another, Raheem began to tear up.

"So, when was you gone tell me this nigga was coming home?" Raheem asked breaking the awkward silence.

"That's what I was tryin' to tell you when I called you over." Deja replied.

"So, I guess we through then, huh?" Raheem snapped. Deja just stood there. She did not know how to reply.

"Obviously, y'all got some things y'all need to talk about. I'ma go upstairs and take a shower." Omar chimed in. He gave Deja a peck on the cheek, and he made his way up the stairs.

"We ain't got shit to talk about! I'm good!" Raheem yelled as he pushed pass Deja and made his way out the door. Deja couldn't take this. She left Omar upstairs, grabbed her keys, jumped in her car, and sped off. *What the fuck just happened I...I didn't mean for things to happen like that. S*he thought to herself. Before Omar's return, she could have her cake and eat it too. Now everything seemed so complicated. She felt like she was forced to make a choice between the two.

Deja drove down Underwood Street with tears streaming down her face. A small part of her was feeling like she may have made the wrong choice. Omar was mature, sexy, and he knew just how to treat a lady. Raheem on the other hand was young, full of excitement, and could fuck Deja like no other. She loved Omar with every piece of her. She knew he loved her too.

After seeing Raheem's reaction, she began to feel something towards him as well. She was torn between the two, and she needed some guidance. Deja pulled over at the stop sign and scrolled through her phone. She needed to talk to somebody, and it didn't matter who the somebody was at this point. As much as she couldn't stand him, she dialed Dominic's number.

"Hello?" Dominic answered with a confused tone.

"Hey Domo. This Deja. What you doin'?" Deja tried to sound as upbeat as possible.

"Hey girl! I ain't doing nothing. Chillin' with Bae and the crew. What's up?" Dominic replied. "I just needed somebody to talk to and honestly you were the only person I could think of. I woulda called Tuesday but you know we ain't cool no mo," Deja said chuckling.

"Aw shit girl. Where you at?" Dominic said with concern.

"I'm on the corner of Andrews and Underwood." Deja replied.

"Oh! You still by the crib. I'm on my way." Dominic said before hanging up.

Dominic walked up to the car about 5

minutes later accompanied by Tuesday.

Oh my God, Deja said to herself. *I'm finna have to fuck this bitch up. Tuesday can't let shit go. I don't feel like beating this bitch ass today.*

"Domo. I said I wanted to talk to you." Deja said as she stepped out the car.

"Bitch anything you gotta say to him, you can say to me." Tuesday snapped.

"Bae...get off that bullshit fa' real. You know I didn't bring you here for that." Dominic said looking at Tuesday.

"If you gone cut up you can take yo dramatic ass right back home." Tuesday just stood there with his arms folded pouting. Deja tried so hard to hold it in, but she giggled. *That shit was funny!* She thought to herself.

"Oh, so you still think shit funny?!" Tuesday yelled as he got in Deja's face.

"Tuesday! What the fuck did I say?" Dominic snapped as he grabbed Tuesday's arm and spun him around.

"Let me go, Domo!" Tuesday shouted as he tussled with Dominic to get away. He was making a huge scene, as usual, people were starting to come out of their houses to catch the action. The situation escalated, and all Deja wanted to do was pour her heart out to somebody.

"I'ma beat that smile right off this bitch's face." Tuesday screamed as he showed out like always, but this time Raheem wasn't here to stop it. "Let me go Domo," Tuesday continually yelled as he finally broke free. "This he-she think he about that life!"

That was all Deja needed to hear. She knocked Tuesday right on his ass and was on top of him like white on rice.

"Is this what you wanted?! I told you not to fuck with me!" Deja screamed as she beat Tuesday in the face. The fight only lasted for a couple of seconds before Dominic broke it up by snatching Deja up. This allowed Tuesday to get up and charge at Deja to retaliate, but it was no use. Dominic stood in between the two of them which made Tuesday lose it.

"Tue! Calm the fuck down!" Dominic screamed.

"Fuck that shit Domo! You let this fuckin' he-she jump on me!" Tuesday screamed as

Dominic held him back. "Y'all know that's a man, right?"

Deja stood there in total shock. She couldn't believe this bitch. Here he was, one wig from being a tranny himself, and he was broadcasting her business to the whole hood. Deja was devastated. She could hear the crowd of people whispering to one another. *That's a man?* She heard one chick say. *I knew it was too good to be true.* She heard another dude say. This shit was unbelievable. This was the whole reason she had left Kentucky, and now the shit was happening right here in her hometown. Deja felt like the world had turned against her, and she had no one to turn to. Deja jumped in her car and sped off.

CHAPTER 14

IN LOVE WITH ANOTHER MAN

"That bitch is a man?" Kiara shouted to her sisters.

"Now that is sum sick shit." One of the sister's said chuckling. Kiara gave her the most piercing pissed off looked. The sister stopped laughing. "I mean...oooh that shit wrong." The sister replied quietly.

"You gone let him choose a nigga ova you?" The other sister asked.

"Not today." Kiara answered. She walked over to Omar's crib and banged on the door.

"The fuck you want, Kiara?" Omar asked as he snatched open the door.

"We need to talk." She said pushing herself passed him and into the house.

"About what?" He asked.

"So you choose a he-she ova me? Really? I thought we really had something! But this...this shit unbelievable!" Tears started streaming down her face. "Was I that bad? Was I that horrible and fucked up that you had to go find some nigga who wanna be a bitch to fuck with?!"

Omar sat quietly on the sofa looking up at her with no remorse.

"Nigga answer me!" Kiara screamed.

"Bitch ion have to answer shit for you or nobody else in this mothafuckin' hood." Omar said standing up. "I don't give a fuck if she was a man, a woman, or a fuckin alien. I want who I want, and I don't want you. SHE is who I want. So take that how you wanna take it. But do that shit on the other side of my doe." Omar said pushing her towards the door.

"Fuck yo fagget ass! I hope you and that Shim catch a fuckin' disease and die!" Kiara ran out the house bawling and screaming causing people to peek out their windows to catch another episode of the hood's drama. She made it back to her apartment and threw herself onto the couch. Omar had been with other chicks before, but this took the cake. *That nigga thinks he's seen the last of me*, she said out loud to the walls.

***

Raheem's rage oozed from his body as he walked back to his crib. *I can't believe this shit,* he said to himself. *How could she do this shit to me?! Everything was goin smooth! She coulda at least told me this nigga was still in the picture! No... This ain't endin' like this. If I can't have her, then nobody will.* He bust through the back door and made his way upstairs. He opened the door to his room and grabbed his gun sitting on the top of his dresser.

As he was headed back out the house, Tuesday stormed into the house with Dominic.

"Where the fuck you goin'? I know not to chase after that bitch." Tuesday shouted.

"Get the fuck outta my way, Tue."
Raheem said pushing Tuesday out of the way. He slammed the door making his way back to Deja's house. On his way to the house, he ran into his homeboy Trent.

"Nigga! You knew Deja was a man?" Trent asked.

"A Man?! Really?" Raheem responded. "I can't believe that shit!"

"Yeah bruh. Him and Tuesday just got to bangin', and Tuesday told everybody. Wait...how your brother knew and didn't tell you?"

"I got somethin' for his ass too...but first...me and Deja gotta talk." Raheem said flashing his pistol. "I'll holla at you later." Raheem dapped up Trent and then continued toward Deja's Crib. *If I can't have you...no one will,* he kept saying to himself.

CHAPTER 15

SAY YES

Tears streamed down Deja's face as she did 100 MPH down Interstate 90. She was determined to get as far away from Rockford as she possibly could. She just didn't know where to go. Deja pulled over and picked up her phone.

"Hello...Saxton's Residence?" A sweet angelic voice answered.

"Hey Momma. It's me." Deja said while sobbing.

"Oh, my lord...it's my baby! Ra'Deja what's wrong baby?" her mother asked concerned.

"I'm sorry I haven't called lately. I just wanted you to know that I'm coming home. Nothing has changed for me. I could have stayed in Louisville for this." Deja cried.

"Well what happened, sweetheart?" Deja proceeded to tell her mother about Omar and Raheem and her encounter with Tuesday.

"Oh sweetie. I'm so sorry that happened. But you didn't know Tuesday was like that. And you didn't know about what Omar was doing. But you knew that getting yourself mixed up with Raheem would have led to that. Be honest."

Deja's crying went to a whimper. "Yeah...I probably shouldn't have done that."

"Grown woman moves come with grown women consequences."

"But Momma...I messed everything up. I didn't mean to cause anyone pain. I didn't mean for all of this to happen. How...How can I make this better, Momma? How can I live with everyone knowing this?"

"I know it's hard, baby. I know it is. But...you gotta live for you and only you. Remember... it's not what you are called. It's what you answer to."

Deja repeated her momma's last words. They were exactly what she needed to get her mind right. Deja didn't need the approval of anybody to be the woman that her mother raised her to be. So, she decided to stay in Rockford. This wasn't going to break her.

"Thank you, Momma. I promise to call more often." Deja said gratefully.

"You welcome, love. Go enjoy yourself. I love you."

"Love you too." Deja hung up the phone and headed back to the FG's. She made it there in no time and everybody was outside. It looked like they were out there waiting on her or something. She instantly spotted Omar in a crowd of people dressed in purple and black talking to a bunch of dudes. He looked so good that Deja wanted to attack him right then and there, but she had to be cautious of how she approached him. She didn't know how quickly word had gotten back to him. If it had, she didn't know how he would react to it. Deja got out of the car and walked up to Omar.

"Can we talk?" She asked nervously.

"Yeah Shorty," he replied with a smile, "But first I got something to say." He grabbed Deja's hand and got on one knee. Deja began to look around. All eyes were on them.

"Omar what are you doin'?" She asked while attempting to cover her mouth and hold back her tears.

"I'm doing what I've wanted to do since the day I laid eyes on you." He replied while pulling a small purple box out of his pocket. "Ra'Deja Shantel Saxton. Will you marry me?" He opened the box to reveal a 5-carat diamond and platinum ring.

"Are you serious?" she asked. The tears that flooded her eyes began to roll down her cheeks.

"All you gotta do is say yes." Omar whispered.

"Yee...." POW! POW! POW!

Deja's response was cut off by 3 gunshots. Screams filled the air as people began to run to the lifeless body that lie on the ground. "Somebody call 911!" A girl screamed out as the blood immediately began to stain the concrete of Fairgrounds.

CHAPTER 16

ROOM 409

"Nooooo!" Deja screamed. "Omar! Omar! Come on! Shit! Omar!" She continued to scream.

"What have I done?" Kiara stood there in complete shock with the smoking gun in her hand. Screams, cries, sirens and flashing lights now filled the air.

"Drop your weapon! Put your hands on your head!" The officers shouted with their guns drawn. Kiara slowly placed the gun on the ground with tears running down her cheeks.

"Put your hands on your head and get down on the ground!" The officers screamed.

"I'm so sorry." Kiara cried as she did what she was told. The officers immediately swarmed

Kiara and placed her in handcuffs. They lifted her off the ground and put her in one of their squad cars.

***

Deja paced back and forth through Rockford Memorial's Emergency Room saturated in blood. She couldn't stop crying, and she was trying to make recall what just happened. All she remembered at the moment was seeing Omar's face as he got down on one knee, and then she heard two or three gunshots go off.

"Excuse me, Ma'am," Deja said frantically to the ER receptionist, "Have you heard anything about Omar Calvary yet?"

The receptionist stopped what she was doing and looked up from her computer. "I know only what I told you the last 10 times you came to the window. He's in surgery, and the doctor will come out and get you when he is back in the recovery room!" She said with a snotty attitude.

Who the fuck did this ole ass bitch think she was talkin' to like that?! Deja thought to herself. If this was under any other circumstance, Deja would have snatched the lady from behind that desk. But at this moment all she could think about was Omar. She needed to see him. She needed to talk to him. She needed to know he was ok. Deja attempted to motivate herself to think positively. *This couldn't be how the story ends! He had just confessed his love to me in front of everybody. Once this was over, we are getting married.* Tears continued to fall from Deja's eyes as she looked down at her 5-carat diamond and platinum engagement ring. *God...if you bring Omar outta this alive, I promise I'll do better. I'll live right. I'll treat people right. I'll even go to church every Sunday. Just please bring him out of this. In Jesus name I pray, Amen!* Leah ran into the waiting room.

"Cuz...I just heard. Are you ok?" Leah whispered hysterically.

"I'm fine. It's Omar." Deja said as she attempted to wipe snot from her runny nose.

"Well, do you know if he's alive? The news said two were shot and one was killed." Leah said with deep concern. Deja jumped up and ran to the reception desk.

"Lady, I need to speak with the doctor takin' care of Omar Calvary, and I need to speak with him now!" Deja demanded.

"That would be me. Are you Deja?" The tall Korean man asked.

"Yes, I am" she replied eagerly.

"I'm Dr. Amaude. Nice to finally meet you." He said shaking Deja's hand.

"Is Omar ok?" she asked?

"Well, the poor guy took two bullets to the chest. They missed his major organs, but he did lose a substantial amount of blood. Once we finally got the bleeding to stop, we had to give him a blood transfusion. He's really lucky to be with us," Dr. Amaude said.

Deja let out a sigh of relief. "Thank you, Jesus! Can I see him?" she asked.

"He needs rest. He's been through a lot, and I don't need him seeing you covered in blood like that. Go home, get cleaned up, and be back here in about an hour or so. By then, the anesthesia should be worn off and then it will be ok to see him." Dr. Amaude explained.

"Ok." Deja replied. She really wanted to see Omar right this instant, but the doctor was right. Omar didn't need to see her like that. So, she took his advice and when home to take a shower.

Deja pulled up to the FG's only to find it looking like a ghost town. There wasn't a soul in sight, and Deja was glad. She didn't feel like explaining what was going on with Omar to anybody. She just wanted to get in the crib, take a shower, and get back to the hospital.

Deja got out the car and made her way to the door, but she couldn't help but notice the massive amount of dried up blood that was in the spot where Omar once laid. A cold chill began to fill her body, but she shook it off and made her way into the crib. *Omar is ok.* She said to herself as she ran up the stairs and hopped in the shower.

Deja's mind began to think back on Leah's words as she stood in the shower and let the water run down her bloodstained body. *Two shot, one killed! Who else got shot?!* Deja asked herself. She grabbed her bodywash and began to quickly scrub the remaining blood off her body. She had to get to Omar. She had to see him for herself.

Deja made it back to the hospital in no time. "Can I speak to Dr. Amaude?" She asked the lady once she made it to the counter. The lady picked up the phone and paged him to the desk. A few minutes went by when the doctor made his way around the corner greeting Deja like he had known her all her life.

"Hey Deja! I was expecting you to come back around this time. The poor guy has been calling out your name ever since he woke up. The anesthesia hasn't completely worn off yet. He's a bit confused, but he is awake. Follow me, and I'll take you up to him." Dr. Amaude answered. Deja was ecstatic. *Omar was callin' out for me,* she thought to herself. She had to be there for him. She had to tell him how much she loved him. Deja briefly looked at her engagement ring while following Dr. Amaude to the room. It was flawless, beautiful, and a perfect fit. *Who would ruin such a perfect moment?* Deja thought.

"Here we are." Dr. Amaude said interrupting Deja's thoughts.

Nervousness began to set in. Hairs on the back of her neck stood up. *What if Omar was in a much worse state than what Dr. Amaude led on?* She thought. Deja took a deep breath, knocked on the door, and walked in the room.

"Omar? Omar? It's me, Deja." She called out quietly. Omar didn't answer. Deja slowly walked up to the bed. She gently pulled the covers from his face. Her heart dropped.

"Raheem?!" Deja exclaimed.

Get Connected with
Author Cordero Diamond
On social media

@corderodiamond1

 @janyiahvscordero

Cordero Diamond

CPSIA information can be obtained
at www.ICGtesting.com
Printed in the USA
LVHW010154260820
664159LV00015B/1182